StoryPlay™

This book belongs to

_____ .

This book was read by

_____

on

_____ .

Are you ready to start reading the **StoryPlay** way?

Read the story on its own. Play the activities together
as you read!

Ready. Set. Smart!

For Michael —
For your wonderful friendship and amazing art! – R.H.H.

For Kieran —
May you never lose anything special again. – M.E.

Library of Congress Cataloging-in-Publication Data available • ISBN 978-1-338-16110-6 • 10 9 8 7 6 5 4 3 2 1   17 18 19 20 21
Printed in Panyu, China   137 • This edition first printing, June 2017 • Book design by Doan Buu
Scholastic Inc, 557 Broadway, New York, NY 10012
Scholastic UK Ltd, Euston House, 24 Eversholt Street, London NW1 1DB

Maybe a BEAR Ate It!

by ROBIE H. HARRIS

illustrated by MICHAEL EMBERLEY

CARTWHEEL BOOKS • NEW YORK • AN IMPRINT OF SCHOLASTIC INC.

What kinds of stuffed animals do you see here?

What's your favorite
bedtime story?

It's gone!

What is gone?

It's nowhere!

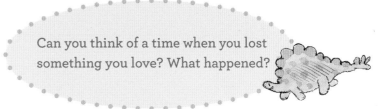

Can you think of a time when you lost something you love? What happened?

I can't find it anywhere!

How does this
character feel?
How do you know?

Where — is — my book?

I need my book!

How does
this character
make YOU feel?

Maybe a

BEAR

ate it!

What sound does the word
BEAR begin with? What
other words start with that
same sound?

How many spikes are
on the dinosaur's tail?
Can you name two other
dinosaurs that have spikes?

Maybe a

STEGOSAURUS

stomped on it!

Maybe a

RHINO

ran away with it!

Maybe a

BAT

flew high up in the sky

with it!

What words rhyme with the word *BAT*?

Where do sharks live?
Can you share two more things you
know about sharks?

Maybe a **SHARK** swallowed it!

What do you think
happened to the book?
How do you know?

Maybe an

ELEPHANT

fell asleep on it!

Well — I can't go to sleep without it!

So I better go look for it!

Looking . . .

I'm looking . . .

I'm still looking . . .

Hey, look!

I found my book!

What makes you
feel happy?

You know what?
I LOVE MY BOOK!

Finish this sentence:
I LOVE MY _____!

Story time fun never ends with these creative activities!

★ Animal Riddles! ★

There are lots of animals in this book—who may or may not have taken THE BOOK! Can you tell them apart from one another? Guess which animal is which by solving these riddles!

1. I'm very big, I weigh a lot, and my teeth are rather scary.
   When creatures see me swimming near, they suddenly get wary.
2. I'm the only mammal who can fly, and my hearing is the best.
   At nighttime I am wide awake. In daytime I'm at rest.
3. I'm the second biggest mammal on land. I have at least one horn.
   I come in several shades of gray. I'm called a calf when I'm born.
4. I'm big and tall, with lots of fur, and in winter I hibernate.
   I spend all summer eating food and gaining lots of weight.
5. I'm the largest mammal on land and weigh much more than a ton.
   I spray water with my long trunk to stay cool in the sun.

Answers can be found at the bottom of the page.

★ Imagination Station ★

When the star of this story loses its favorite book, its imagination runs wild. Have fun using your imagination to finish these sentences—and tell your very own stories!

Once there was a rabbit, a chicken, and a cow who lived on a . . .
Sam was so mad at Henry! Henry couldn't believe his friend would . . .
Bear and Fox always sat next to each other on the bus. But that morning, Fox . . .

[Answers: 1. Shark; 2. Bat; 3. Rhinoceros; 4. Bear; 5. Elephant]